Follow Me

Tricia Tusa

Harcourt Children's Books

Houghton Mifflin Harcourt

Boston   New York   2011

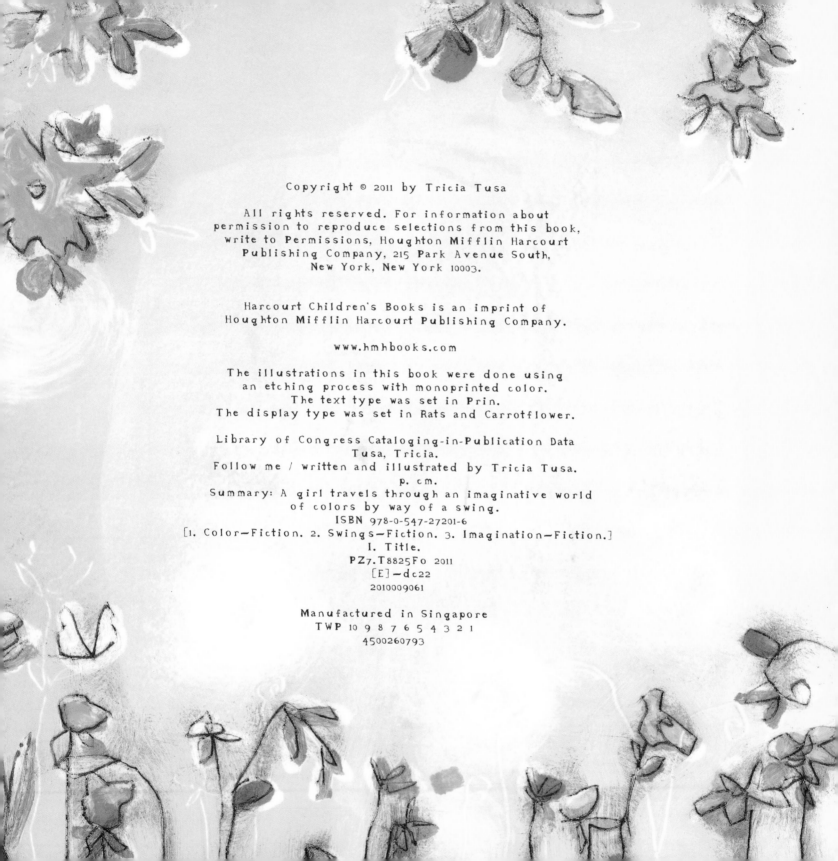

Harcourt Children's Books is an imprint of
Houghton Mifflin Harcourt Publishing Company.

www.hmhbooks.com

The illustrations in this book were done using
an etching process with monoprinted color.
The text type was set in Prin.
The display type was set in Rats and Carrotflower.

Library of Congress Cataloging-in-Publication Data
Tusa, Tricia.
Follow me / written and illustrated by Tricia Tusa.
p. cm.
Summary: A girl travels through an imaginative world
of colors by way of a swing.
ISBN 978-0-547-27201-6
[1. Color—Fiction. 2. Swings—Fiction. 3. Imagination—Fiction.]
I. Title.
PZ7.T8825Fo 2011
[E]—dc22
2010009061

Manufactured in Singapore
TWP 10 9 8 7 6 5 4 3 2 1
4500260793

To childhood, and all that
comes after

I wander through pink

and get lost in blue.

I rise, I fall
in purple and gray.

I whisper, I hum,

and I find my way,

lost in small, green,
happy music.

Follow me, follow me
deep into brown,
into the bright white of yellow,
into orange
that slips into red,

all tumbled together.

Look at me, follow me
into the curl of a breeze.
I am caught
in its folds—

around and around and around.

I reach up,
way out,
over and beyond,

across that easy sway of blue

until

I drift

back

down

down, down

to the green below.

Arms out, head back,
I twirl.

I twirl and I twirl and I twirl

until

I find my way, find my way,

I find my way

back home.